This book belongs to:

_____

¿Where's

El Morro?

Written and illustrated by

Charlene Sánchez

For Cari, Diego, Alejo and Alex.
You guys will always be my inspiration.

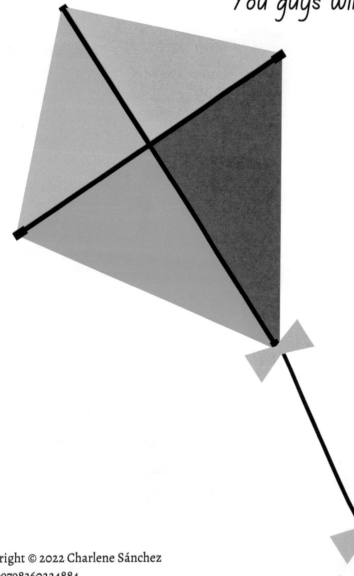
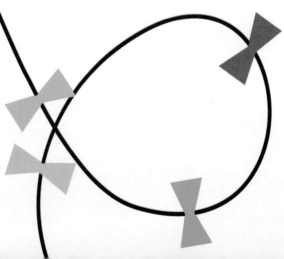

Rani and her grandfather strolled through an Old San Juan street when she suddenly heard in the distance...

El Morro...Rani thought.

"Abuelo, what is El Morro?"

"¡Ah!" her grandfather exclaimed.
"El Morro is very special, Rani."

"You'll know why once you see it."

"Abuelo, is this El Morro?"

"No, Rani", her grandfather said.

"These are **cobblestones**, which are rocks that were placed to protect the streets of Old San Juan from the many tourists and Puerto Ricans that come visit each day."

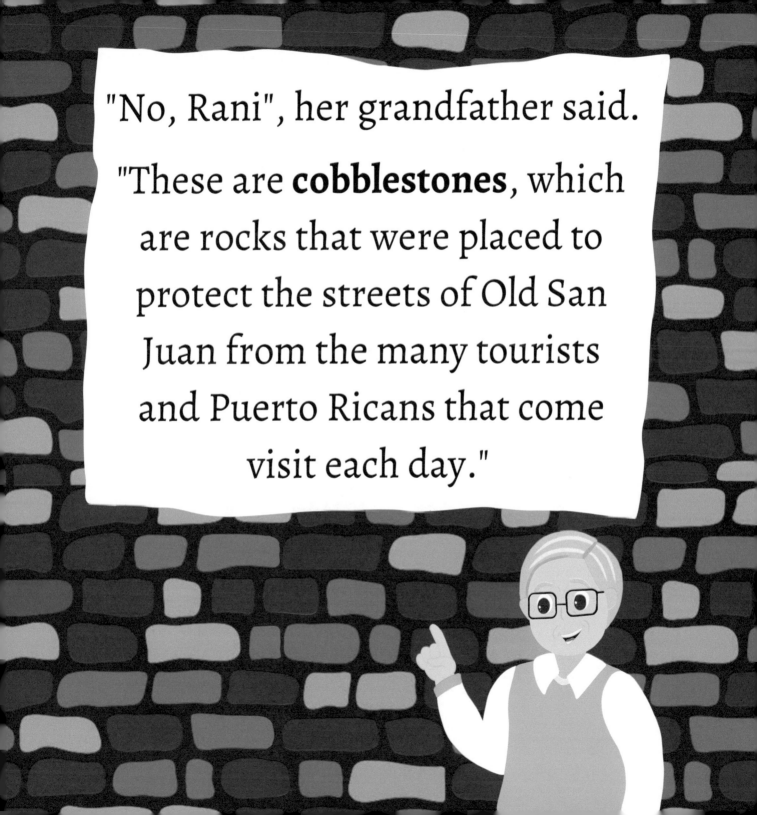

"Abuelo, is this El Morro?"

"No, Rani",
her grandfather said.

"This is called a **garita**. These sentry boxes were used in the past by Spanish soldiers to observe and alert if enemy troops were approaching by sea. There are many located in the walls that surround the city and nowadays are better known as a symbol for the island."

"Abuelo, is this El Morro?"

"No, Rani",
her grandfather said.

"This is **El Parque de las Palomas**."

"A pigeon park where hundreds of pigeons live and are daily fed by anyone that comes to visit them."

"Abuelo, is this El Morro?"

"No, Rani", her grandfather said.

"This is **La Catedral de San Juan Bautista**. It was built in 1521 and is the oldest cathedral in the United States."

"Abuelo, is this El Morro?"

...and so Rani continued her quest to find El Morro while also exploring the streets of Old San Juan.

"Abuelo, is this El Morro?"

"Abuelo, is this El Morro?"

"No, Rani. This is the **Juan Ponce de León** statue. He was Puerto Rico's first governor."

"Abuelo, is this El Morro?"

"No, Rani. This is the **Totem Telúrico**, a sculpture designed by a Puerto Rican artist named Jaime Suárez."

"I'll never find El Morro."
Rani thought to herself when all of a
sudden...

"Abuelo!" Rani exclaimed.

"This is **El Morro!**"

"Very good, Rani. This is **Castillo San Felipe del Morro.** It used to be a fortress built to protect the city of San Juan from sea attacks. Nowadays, its better known as one of the best places to visit and fly kites."

And so Rani finally understood why everyone loved El Morro.

Go back
2 spaces

Move ahead
2 spaces

Lose your
turn

Move back
3 spaces

ve forward
? spaces

Rani needs your help!

Invite your family or friends, grab a dice you could have laying around the house and take turns to see who gets to El Morro first!